. . . it's very, very late,
and I should be sleeping.
But instead, I'm wishing
I were crappie fishing!

My Little Fish House

by Alice Palace

Bearpaw Books

My little fish
house is
made with
lots of stuff,
we collect from
everywhere to make it strong and tough.

We build a little window,
cut in four square holes,
add a stove to keep us toasty,
down to the lake it goes.

Dad takes out the Jiffy auger,
he cleans and shines it up.
He always gets it started,
one pull is just enough!

I finish my presentation,
and drop it down the hole.
I'd like to get my limit,
that will be my goal.

The crappie is a little floppy,
and falls back down the hole.

Looking down that icy tunnel,
we hardly can believe it!
I caught a really big fish,
and no one else will see it.

The sun is going down,
and we pull in our lines.
Walking back to the cabin,
we remember happier times.

Snuggling under my covers,
I wonder what went wrong.

. . . I'm going back to that fishing hole,
to catch the one that got away!

Goodnight Mr. Crappie!

My Little Fish House
Text and Illustrations Copyright 2004 by Alice Sizer
All Rights Reserved

Graphic Design and Illustrations Colorized by Carrie Smeby
Creative Collaboration with Mary Anderson
Technical Assistance by Pamela Costello
"Under The Sea" Photo by Bonita Hein

A Special Thank You To:
In-Fisherman Magazine
Jiffy
Vexilar

ISBN 0-9709444-2-x

For more information contact:
Bearpaw Books
P. O. Box 243
Emily, MN 56447
www.bearpawbooks.com

Enjoy Other Books by Alice Palace:
My Little Cabin
My Little Lighthouse

Printed and Bound in the United States of America by
Daily Printing, Plymouth, Minnesota
Muscle Bound Bindery, Minneapolis, Minnesota